MW00675102

First Edition 2017

For information about special discounts available for
bulk purchases, sales promotions, fund-raising
and educational needs, contact
Diane M. Jackson
at
diane1841@att.net

ISBN 978-0-692-94801-9

How Thelma Got Her Wings

Author: Diane M. Jackson
Illustrator: Andrea Freeman

Note to Young Readers!

As you read, you may run into some words that you do not know. I have italicized and colored some that may be new to you. You may be able to figure them out by the way they are used in the story. If you cannot, then you will have to look them up. If you have a tablet or computer, go to dictionary.com or google the word. You can also ask your parents or big sister or brother to help you with the words. It is important to grow your vocabulary, so have fun with this activity.

peppered
meticulous
recounted
enthralled
stationery
fiscally
retrieve
disastrous
swishing
screeches
turquoise
plops
pondered

Haiti*
astonished
feverishly
Port-au-Prince
whizzing
orphanage
summons
ajitter
rhythms
beckoned
sequined
compassion
donned

* A catastrophic earthquake struck Haiti in 2010 killing over two hundred thousand people leaving many children orphans.

After Thelma's last visit, Zoe could think of nothing else. She *peppered* her grandma with questions at breakfast, on the way to school, everywhere. She wanted to hear about Thelma's visit over and over.

"Grandma, just tell me about Thelma one more time. And start at the beginning and don't leave anything out."

"Zoe, I've told you the story a million times."

"Please, and I promise I won't ask again - Pleeeese, Grandma."

"OKAY, one last time. Deal?"

"Deal!"

And Grandma tells the story of Thelma's visit as Zoe rests her head on Grandma's lap. Grandma describes how Thelma slipped through the window to collect Zoe's tooth from under the pillow. She recalls how Thelma woke her up when she reached under the pillow. Not shy, that sassy tooth fairy introduced herself as Thelma P. Jones.

"She dropped your tooth into her bag and left a message for you, Zoe. Thelma congratulated you on your grades and the *meticulous* care of your teeth. And with that, Zoe, Thelma jumped through the window and hopped into her convertible Mustang waving goodbye as she backed down the driveway."

The whole time Grandma ***recounted*** the story of Thelma, Zoe tried to imagine what Thelma looked like. Grandma told Zoe that Thelma wore jeans, a tee shirt and gym shoes. Zoe had never seen a fairy who looked like that. Zoe was ***enthralled*****.**

"Grandma, do you think Thelma will come back? I have another loose tooth. It's really wiggly. Maybe I will see her this time."

"Well Zoe, you know fairies have a special magic, but tooth fairies can't be seen by children."

"But why, Grandma?"

"It's just one of the rules for tooth fairies."

"It's just not fair, Grandma. I got a lot of questions for Thelma."

"Well then, Zoe, I may have a solution. Why don't you write her a note and leave it with your next tooth?"

"Grandma. I'm going to write that note right now."

Zoe had been pushing the loose tooth with her tongue when it finally dropped into her mouth. She spit it into her hand, examined it, rushed to the bathroom and dropped it into a cup of cold water.

Zoe grabbed her doll Tiffany and ran into her room to search for her favorite purple pen. Opening and slamming drawer after drawer, she finally found the ***stationery*** with the pink hearts. She hugged Tiffany, placed her in the chair near her and settled down with a sigh to write her favorite fairy a note.

Dear Thelma,

Grandma told me all about your visit. I still have the dollar. I put it in my piggy bank. Grandma says I should learn how to save money, that I should be fiscally responsible. I think she means that I should not waste my money.

I sure wish I could meet you, but Grandma explained that you come at night when kids are asleep because we are not supposed to see you. But Grandma told me what you look like, so I can see you in my head.

But Thelma, I have one question I just have to ask you. How did you get your wings? Were you born with them or what? Write me back!

P.S.
I drew a picture of you at the bottom of this note. Tell me if you like it!

Love,

Zoe

Zoe carefully folded the note and put it in an envelope. As she started to lick the envelope, she suddenly remembered her tooth. She ran into the bathroom to ***retrieve*** her tooth and checked to make sure that it was clean. Zoe dropped the tooth into the envelope and wrote on the front -

To: Miss Thelma P. Jones,
Tooth Fairy
Private!

"Now where should I leave this note?" Zoe ***pondered***.

"I got it!" She placed the envelope in the hallway on the floor right outside of her bedroom.

Birthday
7

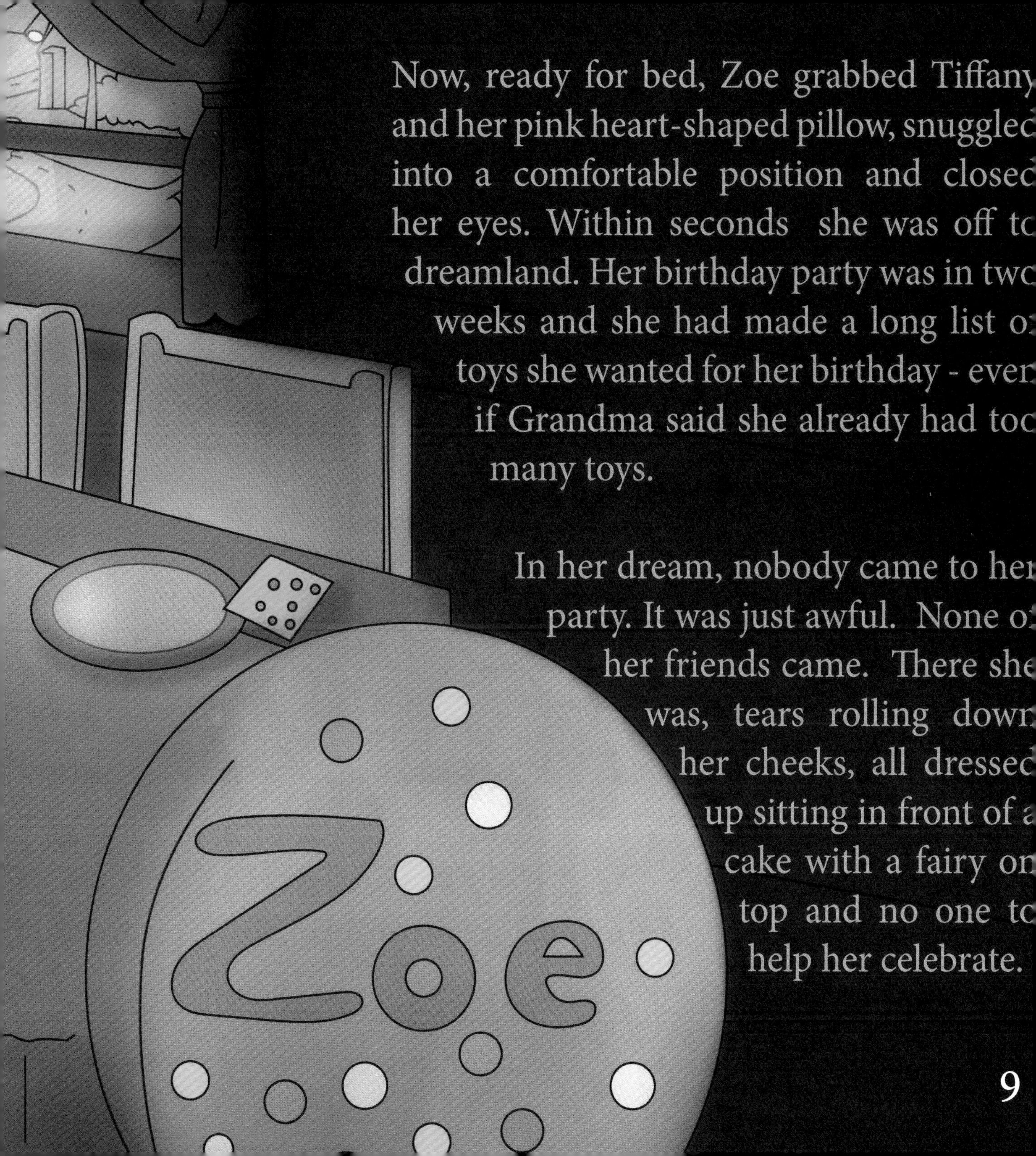

Now, ready for bed, Zoe grabbed Tiffany and her pink heart-shaped pillow, snuggled into a comfortable position and closed her eyes. Within seconds she was off to dreamland. Her birthday party was in two weeks and she had made a long list of toys she wanted for her birthday - even if Grandma said she already had too many toys.

In her dream, nobody came to her party. It was just awful. None of her friends came. There she was, tears rolling down her cheeks, all dressed up sitting in front of a cake with a fairy on top and no one to help her celebrate.

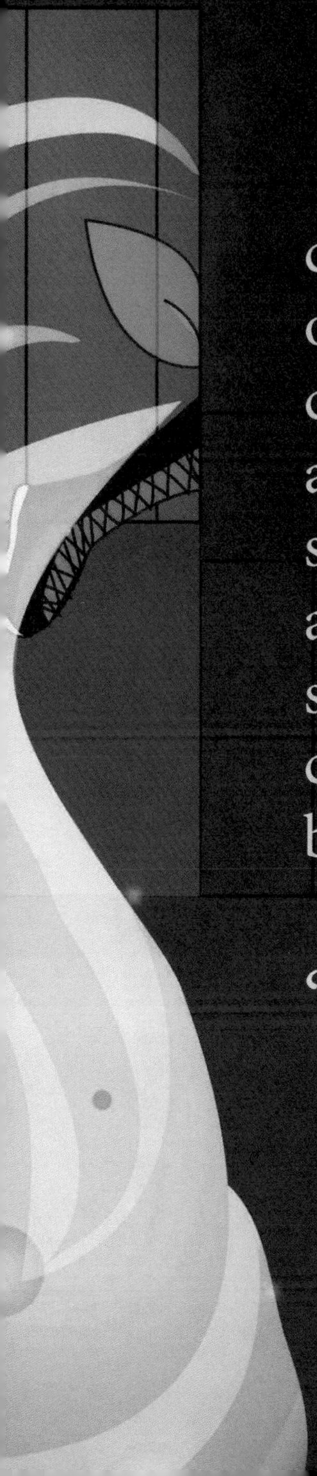

"But Mommy, how come no one came to my party? This is the worst day of my life." Mom tried, but there was no comforting Zoe. Her birthday party was a disaster. As she sat there removing the seven candles from the cake, she heard a ***swishing*** sound just behind her right shoulder. As she turned to see what had caused the strange sound, her Mom's voice broke through her dream.

"Zoe, it's time to get up."

It took Zoe a few minutes to realize that her ***disastrous*** birthday party had all been a terrible dream. But she was curious; what had caused that ***swishing*** sound just before her dream was interrupted?

"I guess I'll never know," Zoe mumbles as she throws back the covers and swings one foot onto the carpet. Still sleepy, she starts to the bathroom across the hall. Then she sees it.

"Oh my God!" Zoe ***screeches*** as she rushes to pick up and open the familiar tiny green treasure box. The letter she wrote Thelma was gone.

Thelma had been here!

Now wide awake, Zoe searched the treasure box - no dollar bill. Instead, a tiny ***turquoise*** square was stuffed into the box. Curious, Zoe removes the paper from the treasure box and unfolds it.

Zoe runs to Grandma's room yelling, "Grandma, look, look what Thelma left me. She left me a letter."

"What does the letter say?" Grandma asked.

"I haven't read it yet."

"What are you waiting on, girl?"

Zoe ***plops*** onto Grandma's bed and begins reading.

Fairies Rule
XOXO Thelma

Dear Zoe,

The tooth looks good. Do you go to the dentist for check ups? You must be brushing before you go to bed. Good job!

Now to your question: How did I get my wings? First of all, I was born with a tiny set of wings, but the ones Grandma saw were a gift. You see, I love kids and when I saw pictures of kids in ***Haiti*** after the earthquake, I wrote some of my fairy friends asking them to help me with a project.

Fairies
Rock!

Packing Party
for Haiti

I was ***astonished*** when so many of my friends replied that they wanted to participate in a project that would bring a little joy to children who had lost so much.

We collected toys, tee shirts, toothbrushes, little bottles of water and books which we stuffed into book bags. Cindy, my best friend, suggested that we write notes to the children, too. We worked ***feverishly*** collecting donations and stuffing backpacks. We could hardly wait to start our journey.

Fairies
Rock!

During one particularly bright night, the sky dotted with millions of tiny stars, we took off to ***Port-au-Prince.*** That night we did not collect teeth. We were on a different mission. Imagine tooth fairies with sacks full of gifts ***whizzing*** through the night skies .

Fairies Rock!

When we reached the ***orphanage***, we circled to slow down and landed on a balcony. Peeping through the windows, we spotted the children asleep on cots.

Careful not to wake them, we climbed through the open windows and placed backpacks next to the children's cots.

Fairies
Rock!

Once done, we climbed back out the windows, checked out the night sky and took off with the moon lighting our way.

We giggled all the way back home. We could just imagine the children's surprise as they awoke and found their backpacks filled with goodies.

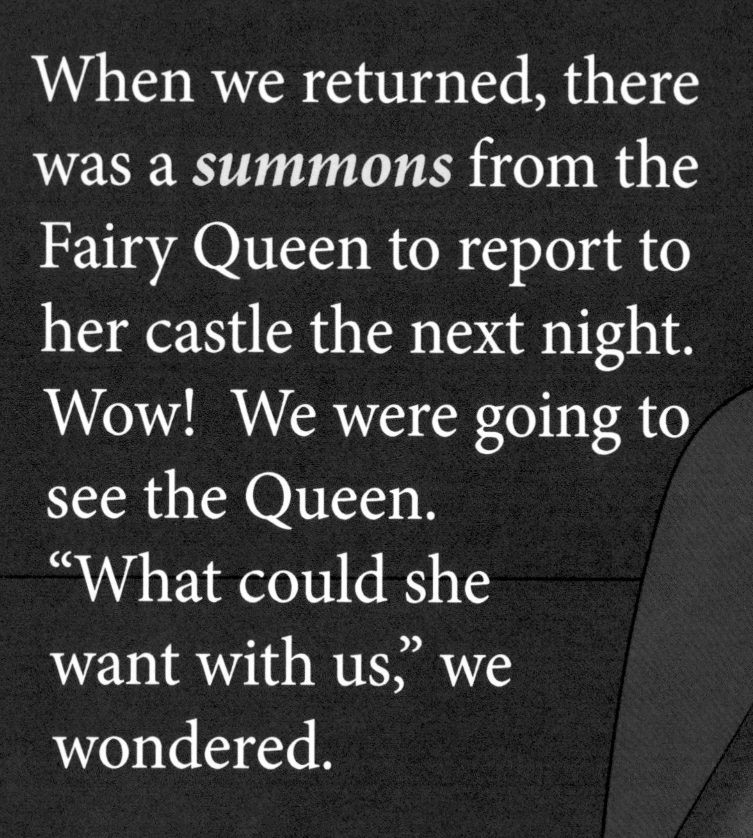

When we returned, there was a ***summons*** from the Fairy Queen to report to her castle the next night. Wow! We were going to see the Queen. “What could she want with us,” we wondered.

All a *ajitter*, we flew to the castle. Even before we entered, we could hear the *rhythms* of a jazz band welcoming us.

"What do you suppose is going on tonight?" Marly whispered.

"I don't know, but I am glad we got invitations," Sepia giggled.

"Well, let's get this party started." I grinned as I led the way into the banquet hall.

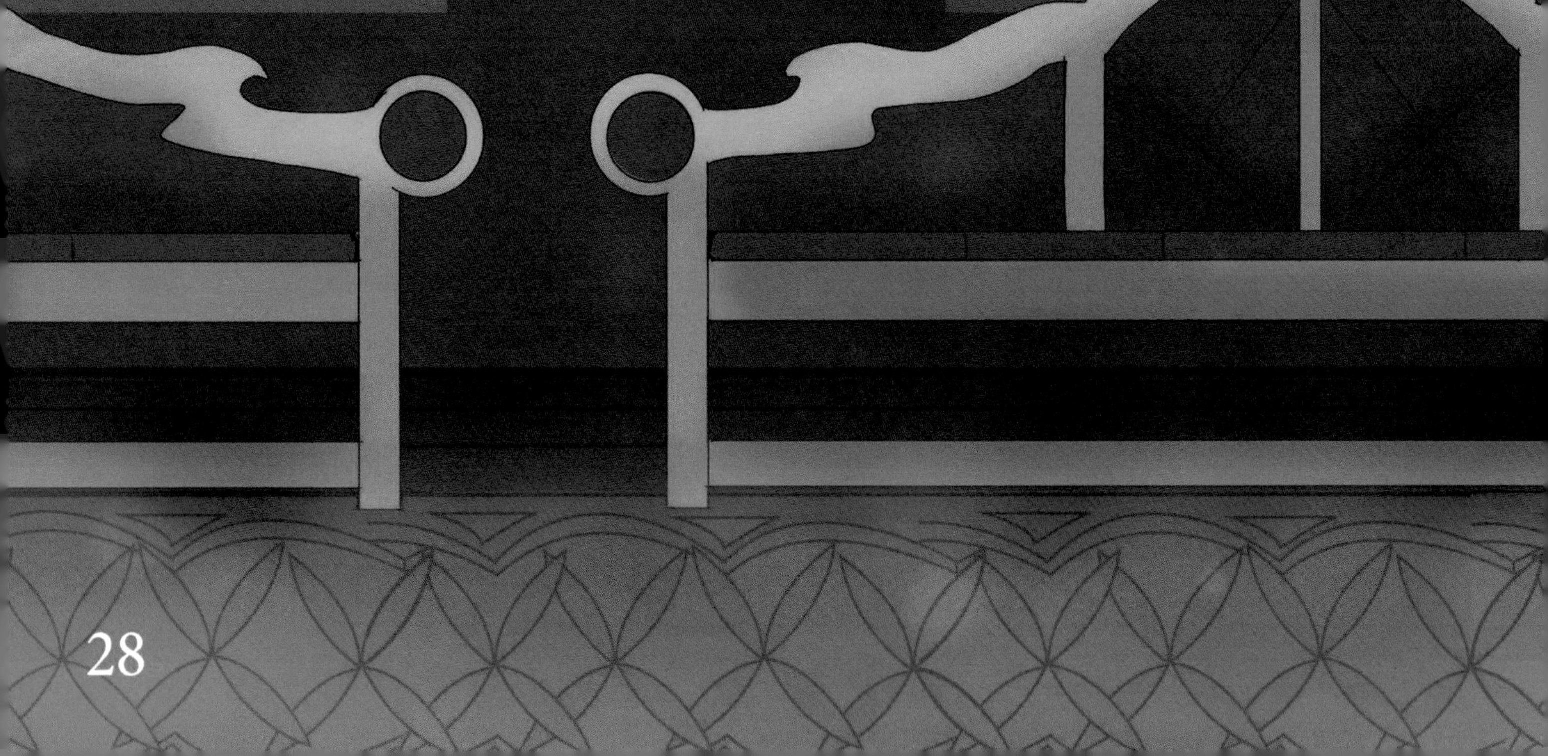

Queen Winnie, standing in front of her throne, welcomed us.

"Come in little fairies. You are our very special guests tonight."

"This is all for us, Queen Winnie?" Marly asked.

Queen Winnie smiled and ***beckoned*** us to join her in front of a dazzling throne surrounded by her fairy court.

Queen Winnie then pulled out of her ***sequined*** bag the most beautiful wings I had ever seen.

"I am so proud of what you fairies did for the children in Haiti. You demonstrated love and caring to those who had suffered a terrible loss. Because of your wonderful work, I am presenting each of you with new wings. May these wings remind you of the love and ***compassion*** you showed others. Wear them and continue to look out for those who need a helping hand. Yes, the work you do collecting teeth is very important. Continue to do that, but always find time in your schedules for love."

Tears flowed from my eyes. As Sepia sniffled, I saw Carly wiping tears away. Never did we expect to receive any recognition for what we had done. We were just happy to bring joy to some kids who had had a very rough time. Most had lost their homes, friends and families. Ours was a small token of love.

One by one, we received our wings. Zoe, my wings are turquoise and lavender with tiny bells that jingle when I move. Marly's wings are an amazing green, and Sepia's are black with silver stars.

Once we ***donned*** our new wings, we joined the other guests and danced the night away. I will never forget that night.

So, there it is, Zoe, the story of how I got my wings. I hope that answers your question, Miss Curious.

Love and Kisses,
Thelma P. Jones

P.S. Zoe, I try to be very quiet on my tooth collections, but I was rushing last night when I ran by your room. I hope I didn't wake you, but if you heard a strange noise, it might have been me.

Reading Rules!

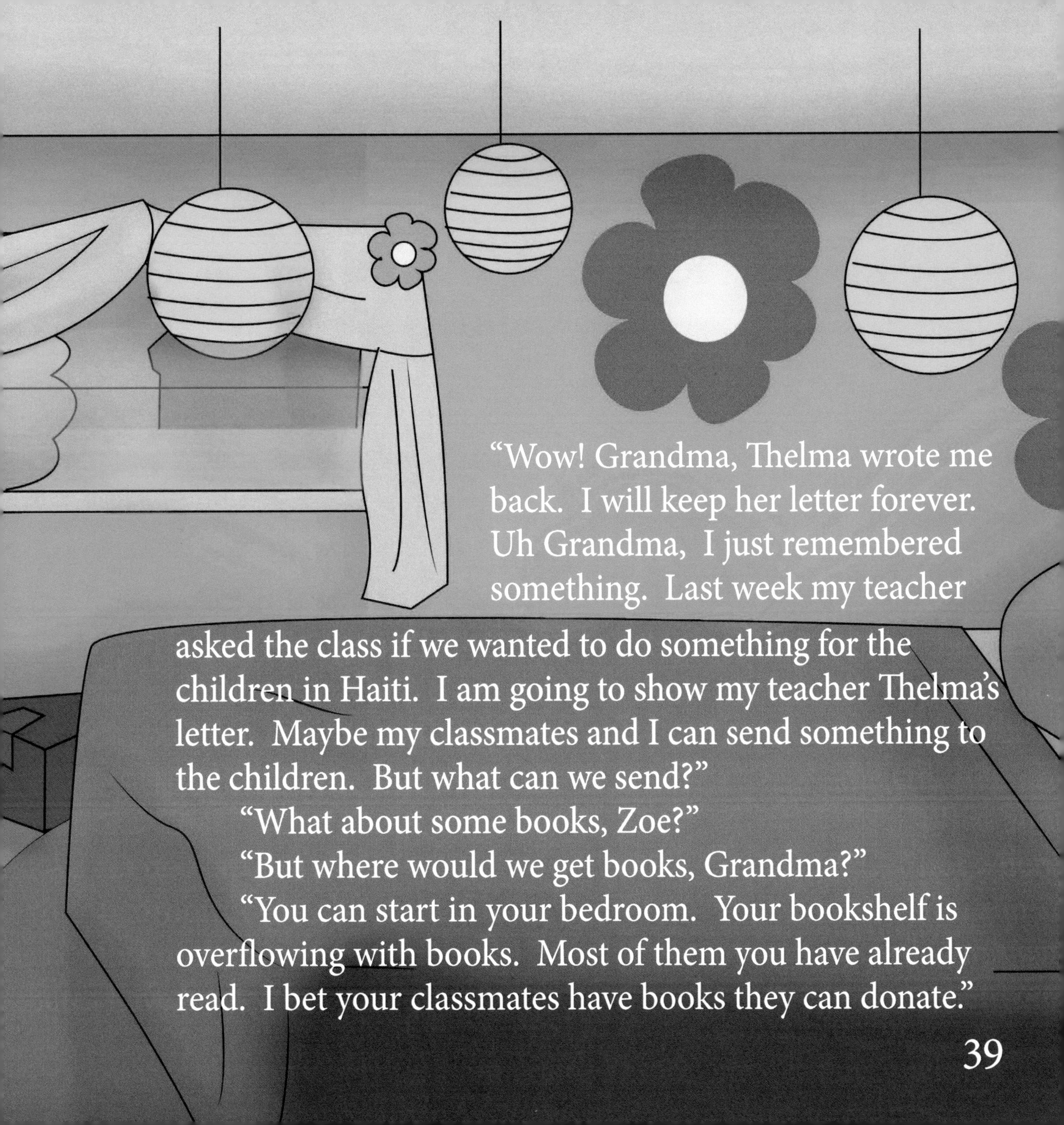

"Wow! Grandma, Thelma wrote me back. I will keep her letter forever. Uh Grandma, I just remembered something. Last week my teacher asked the class if we wanted to do something for the children in Haiti. I am going to show my teacher Thelma's letter. Maybe my classmates and I can send something to the children. But what can we send?"

"What about some books, Zoe?"

"But where would we get books, Grandma?"

"You can start in your bedroom. Your bookshelf is overflowing with books. Most of them you have already read. I bet your classmates have books they can donate."

"Grandma, I think I heard Thelma last night. I thought it was a dream, but it was Thelma. Ooh Grandma, I can't wait to tell Mrs. Richards about our plan. What time is it anyway? It must be time for school."

"Well Missy, you aren't usually so eager to get to school."

"I'm on a mission today; so let's go, Grandma."

"Okay little girl, get dressed and let's go."

In record time Zoe had brushed her teeth, made her bed, put on her uniform and eaten her breakfast.

"Grandma, do you think I will get wings like Thelma?'

"No, Zoe, you won't get wings, but you will get something even better."

"What's better than wings, Grandma?"

"The joy you get from knowing that you have done something wonderful."

"Really, Grandma?"

"Really, Zoe."

Growing up in an era when textbooks and children's literature included no images of African American characters, Diane Jackson wanted to provide an experience for children of the world, one that she had been denied. Her granddaughter, Zoe, who had just lost a tooth was expecting a visit from the tooth fairy. But, Jackson would give her granddaughter a surprise. Her tooth fairy would be black and beautiful and a citizen of the world. It was then that Thelma P. Jones was born, at least in her imagination. In collaboration with her illustrator Andrea Freeman, Thelma P. Jones was born and ready to tell her story.

The author is currently residing in Lansing, Illinois enjoying her retirement from the classroom. Having taught English/Language Arts for over forty years, she now spends her time reading, writing and telling stories. Diane Jackson began her teaching career in Chicago, then after completing her Masters in the Art of Teaching from the University of Chicago, she relocated to California where she taught English in Compton and Los Angeles. As department chair, she helped to develop curriculum supported by best practices that would engage the imaginations of her students. Her professional career was highlighted by her National Board for Professional Teaching Standards Certification in Adolescent and Young Adult Language Arts. Additionally, she attended the UCLA Writing Workshop - twice- which would impact her ability to develop the writer in her students and find the writer in herself.

Andrea Freeman is a Chicago based artist and illustrator that enjoys creating imaginative illustrations geared towards children and adults alike. As a child she doodled as a means of battling shyness – but soon it turned into a passion and enjoyable experience to share with others.

When not creating the magical world of Thelma and friends – Andrea enjoys crafting and working at Artreach Chicago; an organization that provides satellite art programming to underserved communities in Chicago, as well as art therapy to youth affected by gun violence.

She hopes to one day facilitate a studio space for artists of all backgrounds to have full access to the resources and support needed to create and grow as artists.

You can find more of her work at:
afreeman5566.wixsite.com/portfolio

For all further inquiries she can be reached via her website ***afreeman5566.wixsite.com/portfolio*** or at ***afreeman5566@gmail.com***.